3800 16 0074087 6

HIGH LIFE HIGHLAND

D1187253

HIGH LIFE HIGHLAND LIBRARIES	
38001600740876	
BERTRAMS	02/12/2016
	£3.99
JF	

Published 2015 by Geddes & Grosset, an imprint of The Gresham
Publishing Company Ltd, Academy Park, Building 4000,
Gower Street, Glasgow, G51 1PR, Scotland

First published 1997. Reprinted 2006, 2015.

Copyright © 1997 The Gresham Publishing Company Ltd

All rights reserved. No part of this publication may be reproduced,
stored in a retrieval system or transmitted in any form or by
any means, electronic, mechanical, photocopying, recording or
otherwise, without the prior permission of the copyright holder.

Conditions of Sale:
This book is sold with the condition that it will not, by way of trade
or otherwise, be resold, hired out, lent, or otherwise distributed or
circulated in any form or style of binding or cover other than that
in which it is published and without the same conditions being
imposed on the subsequent purchaser.

Written by Judy Hamilton.
Artwork by Mimi Everett, courtesy of Simon Girling & Associates,
Hadleigh, Suffolk.

ISBN 978-1-910680-56-8

Printed and bound in Malaysia

Susie & Sam

Go to
the
Museum

Geddes & Grosset

It was Saturday afternoon and Susie and Sam were very fed up. It had been raining all morning and they couldn't get out to play in the garden. They had played in the house all morning and now they were getting bored.

Mum and Dad were in the sitting room reading the newspapers. Susie and Sam went in to see them.

"There's nothing to do!" grumbled Sam.

"It's a horrible day and we're bored!" complained Susie.

Dad and Mum looked at each other and sighed.

"I think this rain is making us all fed up," said Dad. "How about a trip to the museum to cheer us up?"

"Ben says the museum is boring," said Sam.

"Ben doesn't know everything," said Mum. "We haven't been to the museum since you were very small and I think that you and Susie will like it. It's certainly better than staying inside and grumbling!"

A little later, Susie, Sam, Mum and
Dad were climbing the steps leading up
to the door of the museum. It was a huge
building. Inside, there was a great big
hall full of statues and glass cases. There
were doorways all round the hall leading
to other rooms in the museum.

II

"Where shall we start?" said Dad. He
looked at the big sign on the wall to find
out what there was to see.

"Does anyone here like dinosaurs?" he
asked.

"We do!" said Susie and Sam.

"Right then, come on!" said Dad.
"There's a special exhibition over this
way!"

The dinosaur exhibition was wonderful.
There were models of all the dinosaurs
that Susie and Sam had heard of, and lots
more besides. There were real dinosaur
bones and teeth to look at.

There were computers in the room as well and Mum and Dad helped Susie and Sam to use them. Dad and Susie did a dinosaur quiz on their computer. Mum and Sam had fun making different dinosaur noises with theirs.

When they had finished looking at the dinosaur exhibition, Mum and Dad took them into another hall.

"Look up!" said Mum.

Susie and Sam looked up. Hanging from the roof was the biggest skeleton they could ever imagine.

"What is it?" said Sam.

"It's a whale skeleton," said Dad. "I bet you didn't think whales could ever be this big!"

"Is it safe up there?" said Susie.

"Don't worry, Susie," said Dad. "It's hanging on good, strong wires."

16

Stuffed animals and birds of all kinds of different shapes and sizes were positioned all round the hall.

In one corner of the room was a big tiger, with its teeth showing in a fierce snarl.

"It looks as if it's still alive!" said Sam.

19

When they had finished looking at all the animals, they went to another room to see a display of clothes that people used to wear a long time ago. Susie thought that some of the dresses that women used to wear looked beautiful.

"I would like a dress like that!" she said, pointing one out to Mum.

"I don't think dresses like that were very comfortable to wear," said Mum. "Just imagine trying to ride your bike wearing all those petticoats!"

There was still plenty more to see. They went to look at a display of model steam engines and had fun pressing buttons to make them work.

They saw coins from ancient Rome, precious vases from China and mummies from Egypt. They saw an exhibition of soldiers' uniforms, some from long ago and some from modern times.

They also saw all kinds of different musical instruments from countries all over the world.

Some of the instruments were locked safely inside glass cases, but there were some that had been put out for people to try.

Susie and Sam had lots of fun playing with some hand bells and a glockenspiel.

"What a noise!" said Dad, putting his fingers in his ears.

After a while, Susie and Sam began to feel tired.

"Time to go home for dinner," said Mum.

"But we haven't finished looking at everything yet!" said Sam.

"There's too much to see all in one day," said Dad. "But we can come back another day if you like. Would you like that?"

"Yes, please!" said Susie and Sam.